Ideas, Inventions, and Innovators

THE GREATEST HUMAN
ACHIEVEMENTS

BY GRACE JONES & KIRSTY HOLMES

CRABTREE
PUBLISHING COMPANY
WWW.CRABTREEBOOKS.COM

CRABTREE
PUBLISHING COMPANY
WWW.CRABTREEBOOKS.COM

Published in Canada
Crabtree Publishing
616 Welland Avenue
St. Catharines, ON
L2M 5V6

Published in the United States
Crabtree Publishing
PMB 59051
350 Fifth Ave, 59th Floor
New York, NY 10118

Published in 2019 by Crabtree Publishing Company

Author: Grace Jones & Kirsty Holmes

Editorial director: Kathy Middleton

Editors: Holly Duhig, Petrice Custance

Proofreader: Melissa Boyce

Designer: Gareth Liddington

Prepress technicians: Tammy McGarr, Ken Wright

Print coordinator: Katherine Berti

Images

Shutterstock: Anton_Ivanov p 5 (2nd row, middle); Rob Crandall p 7
(bottom); Dmitry Birin p 9 (top); S-F p 15 (top); Petr Toman p 20 (left);
catwalker p 23 (left, middle)

Wikimedia: title page; p 5 (bottom right); p 6 (bottom); p 7 (top); p 8
(bottom); p 9; p 11 (top); p 12, p 13 (top); p 14; p 15 (bottom); p 16;
p 17 (top, middle); p 18 (bottom left); p 20 (bottom right); p 21; p 22
(left); p 24 (bottom); p 25 (bottom); p 26 (bottom left, right); pp 27–29;

All facts, statistics, web addresses and URLs in this book were verified
as valid and accurate at time of writing. No responsibility for any
changes to external websites or references can be accepted by either
the author or publisher.

Printed in the U.S.A./122018/CG20181005

Library and Archives Canada Cataloguing in Publication

Jones, Grace, 1990-, author
        The greatest human achievements / Grace Jones, Kirsty Holmes.

(Ideas, inventions, and innovators)
Includes index.
Issued in print and electronic formats.
ISBN 978-0-7787-5827-3 (hardcover).--
ISBN 978-0-7787-5969-0 (softcover).--
ISBN 978-1-4271-2238-4 (HTML)

        1. Curiosities and wonders--Juvenile literature. 2. Successful
people--Juvenile literature. I. Holmes, Kirsty, author II. Title.

AG244.J66 2018   j031.02   C2018-905462-X
                                                                        C2018-905463-8

Library of Congress Cataloging-in-Publication Data

Names: Jones, Grace, 1990- author. | Holmes, Kirsty, author.
Title: The greatest human achievements / Grace Jones, Kirsty Holmes.
Description: New York : Crabtree Publishing Company, [2019] |
    Series: Ideas, inventions, and innovators | Includes index.
Identifiers: LCCN 2018043642 (print) | LCCN 2018046522 (ebook) |
    ISBN 9781427122384 (Electronic) |
    ISBN 9780778758273 (hardcover) |
    ISBN 9780778759690 (pbk.)
Subjects: LCSH: History--Miscellanea--Juvenile literature.
Classification: LCC D24 (ebook) | LCC D24 .J66 2019 (print) |
    DDC 904/.7--dc23
LC record available at https://lccn.loc.gov/2018043642

CONTENTS

THE GREATEST HUMAN ACHIEVEMENTS

Over thousands of years, humans have achieved many extraordinary **feats**, from dreaming up mind-boggling inventions to making groundbreaking discoveries and even traveling to outer space. Inventors, artists, scientists, and astronauts are just some of the people whose accomplishments have inspired millions of people and changed the world forever.

Why is democracy important?

How long was the flight of the first piloted airplane?

Who were the first people to climb the highest mountain?

Who left the first footprints on the Moon?

What was special about this ceiling?

Who won the race to the ends of the Earth?

Who discovered our connection to the apes?

Who was the first person to run a mile in less than four minutes?

Who invented the telephone?

How are we able to prevent hundreds of diseases?

Who caught us all in the World Wide Web?

What human-made object has traveled the farthest in space?

Let's go on a journey to find the answers to these questions and more...

DEMOCRACY

Some of the greatest human achievements can be measured in numbers and distances, such as climbing the tallest mountain in the world or scoring a perfect 10 at the Olympics. Democracy is different. It is a system of government as well as a way of life. One of the most important **principles** of democracy is freedom.

The word democracy comes from a Greek word meaning rule by the people. Athens, Greece is considered the birthplace of democracy. More than 2,500 years ago, citizens of Athens developed a system of government in which citizens had a say in how the government was run, through voting. Democracy has since spread to many parts of the world, including Europe, North America, and South America.

The Declaration of Independence, signed by the Founding Fathers of the United States in 1776, lists several principles of democracy, including equality and freedom.

2016 meeting of leaders from the world's largest democracies, including the United States, Canada, Japan, Germany, France, Italy, and the United Kingdom.

Democracy is important because it offers people freedom of choice. In countries that are not democracies, such as **dictatorships**, citizens have very little freedom and do not have a say in how their country is run. Citizens of non-democratic countries, such as North Korea, often live in extreme hardship, and risk jail or even death for daring to speak against their government.

In democracies such as the United States and Canada, citizens have the freedom to express themselves and to speak out when they disagree with their government. Citizens of democracies vote for their government representatives and have a say in how their country is run.

The health of a democracy depends on its citizens exercising their right to vote.

FLYING THROUGH THE SKIES

At 10:35 a.m. on December 17, 1903, just south of Kitty Hawk, North Carolina, two brothers named Orville and Wilbur Wright made the very first flight in a piloted, engine-powered airplane.

The Wright brothers' aircraft was called the *Wright Flyer*. It is considered to be the very first successful airplane. The Wright brothers' first flight covered 120 feet (37 meters) and lasted 12 seconds. Later that same day, they flew the *Wright Flyer* a distance of 852 feet (260 meters) for 59 seconds.

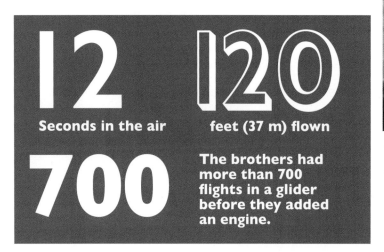

12
Seconds in the air

120
feet (37 m) flown

700
The brothers had more than 700 flights in a glider before they added an engine.

The two brothers decided who would fly the plane first by a coin toss. Wilbur won, but crashed his attempt. A few days later, Orville had his turn and became the first person ever to successfully fly an airplane!

The *Wright Flyer*

After their first successful flight, the Wright brothers started the Wright Company. Their factory in Dayton, Ohio was the first built in the U.S. for the purpose of manufacturing airplanes.

By changing the way people travel, Orville and Wilbur Wright changed the world. Trips that at one time took months by boat or train are now traveled by air in just a few hours. Today, the airline industry employs nearly 10 million people around the world.

The Wright brothers also provided the first vital step in traveling beyond our world. During the first Moon landing in 1969, Neil Armstrong took a part of the *Wright Flyer* with him on his very own historic flight.

Flight Attendant

Neil Armstrong

CLIMBING MOUNT EVEREST

On May 29, 1953, Edmund Hillary from New Zealand and **Sherpa** Tenzing Norgay from Nepal were the first people to reach the **summit** of Mount Everest. Mount Everest is in the Himalayan mountain range in Nepal. It is the tallest mountain peak in the world.

In March 1953, around 400 members started on the **expedition** to reach the 29,029-foot (8,848-m) summit. They climbed the mountain in stages, moving to a higher camp every few weeks to get used to the high **altitudes**. At 11:30 a.m. on May 29, Hillary and Norgay reached the tallest point on Earth.

29,029
feet (8,848 m) high

In Nepalese, the mountain is called Sagarmatha, which means "goddess of the sky."

60
60 million years old

Mount Everest

Modern climbers with new equipment

Before finally reaching the summit, Hillary and Norgay faced a 39-foot (12-m) near-vertical rock face, named afterward "the Hillary Step." An earthquake in 2015 caused much of the Hillary Step to crumble away, making the final climb to the summit now a little easier.

The Hillary Step

-2 °F

The average summer temperature on Mount Everest is -2 °F (-19 °C).

175

The highest recorded wind speed at the summit is 175 miles per hour (282 kph).

Since Sir Edmund Hillary and Tenzing Norgay reached the summit, there have been over 7,600 climbs of Mount Everest by over 4,450 different people. Many people, often Sherpas, have since reached the peak of Mount Everest, which is still considered a very difficult climb.

The youngest person to reach the summit was 13-year-old American Jordan Romero in 2010. Eighty-year-old Yuichiro Miura, from Japan, became the oldest person to reach the summit in 2013.

LANDING ON THE MOON

On July 20, 1969, people around the world turned on their television sets to watch the impossible. Three astronauts—Neil Armstrong, Edwin "Buzz" Aldrin, and Michael Collins—landed a manned rocket ship on the Moon for the first time.

Just four days earlier, the astronauts were launched into space and history on a mission known as Apollo 11. Their spacecraft traveled 240,000 miles (386,000 km) to reach the Moon's surface. At 10:56 p.m. on July 20, with more than half a billion people watching on television, Neil Armstrong took the first human step onto a surface beyond Earth.

Apollo 11 launch

240,000
miles (386,000 km) traveled

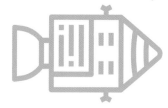

363-foot (111-m) rocket

3
Astronauts

All the meals that the astronauts ate had to be lightweight and small so that they didn't weigh down the rocket. The first meal that Neil Armstrong ate after landing on the Moon was apparently bacon cubes!

While Michael Collins stayed inside the rocket ship, Neil Armstrong and Buzz Aldrin explored the Moon's surface, taking photographs and collecting samples to take back to Earth. They also left behind an American flag, parts of the *Wright Flyer*, and a message reading "Here men from the planet Earth first set foot upon the Moon, July 1969 A.D. We came in peace for all mankind."

Did you know that the four-billion-year-old dust on the Moon's surface has an odor? Neil Armstrong described it as smelling like "wet ashes in a fireplace."

The Apollo 11 team inspired a whole generation to dream about the possibilities of space. Since then, humans have achieved amazing advancements in space travel and technology. A colony on Mars in the not-too-distant future is now a possibility. This would not even have been thought possible before Collins, Aldrin, and Armstrong landed on the Moon.

"That's one small step for a man, one giant leap for mankind."
Neil Armstrong's famous words, broadcast live around the world, as he stepped onto the Moon's surface.

13

PAINTING THE SISTINE CHAPEL

The Sistine **Chapel** is a famous chapel in Vatican City, near Rome, Italy. It is the seat of the pope, or the head of the **Roman Catholic** church. The inside of the chapel is decorated with many beautiful paintings, known as **frescoes**. The most famous part of the Sistine Chapel is its very special ceiling.

Michelangelo

In 1508, Pope Julius II asked the famous artist, Michelangelo, to paint the chapel's ceiling. Michelangelo originally turned down the work, saying he was a **sculptor** and not a painter, but eventually agreed. He built a **scaffold** to allow him to complete the painting, and created one of the most important works of art ever accomplished. The painting took four years to complete.

The Creation of Adam, part of the Sistine chapel ceiling, is one of the most famous paintings in the world.

Part of the Sistine Chapel ceiling

Twenty-two years after painting the ceiling, Michelangelo returned to the Sistine Chapel to paint a huge fresco on the wall behind the altar. *The Last Judgement*, shown below, took him six years to complete.

To paint these incredible works of art, Michelangelo built a huge scaffold, and stood up on it to paint. He later wrote a poem explaining how hard the work was, reaching above his head to paint every day for many years. He painted onto a wet plaster surface, which smelled terrible and made him feel ill.

What Michelangelo created in the Sistine Chapel is considered to be one of the greatest artistic achievements of all time. People travel from all over the world to marvel at what one man was able to do.

The Last Judgement

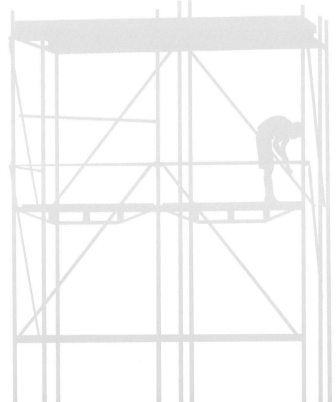

15

TO THE ENDS OF THE EARTH

The ends of the Earth are the North and South Poles, which are the most northern and southern points of the world. Humans have only quite recently been able to reach these extreme locations—but who were the first people to achieve this extraordinary feat?

THE SOUTH POLE

The South Pole is located on the continent of Antarctica. It is a very **barren** place, completely surrounded by ice and snow, with extreme cold temperatures. It is very difficult to reach the South Pole, although this didn't stop many people from trying. In 1901, Robert Falcon Scott and his team attempted to reach it, but were forced to turn back. In 1911, Norwegian explorer Roald Amundsen, and a party of four others, set out to reach the South Pole and, walking the final part of the journey across the ice, reached it on December 14, 1911. They pitched a tent and were the first to mark the location of the South Pole, making history as they did so.

The Ceremonial South Pole, surrounded by flags of the countries who have agreed to keep it safe and **neutral**.

THE NORTH POLE

Many people have claimed to be the first, but as the North Pole is on floating ice, it is harder to be sure who exactly was the first to set foot there.

Frederick Albert Cook claimed to have reached the North Pole in 1908, but later lost his papers and could not prove his claim. Cook had a photograph which he said was taken at the North Pole, and he stood by his story until his death.

Robert Peary

In 1909, Rear Admiral Robert Peary also claimed to have reached the North Pole. A difficult expedition led most of Peary's team to turn back. He pressed on with only a small team of assistants. Peary claims he reached the North Pole, but there are many who doubt his claim.

This is Peary's diary entry when he **allegedly** reached the Pole.

In 1969, British explorer Sir Walter "Wally" Herbert walked to the North Pole (and proved it!). He was **knighted** for his achievements, and has a mountain range and **plateau** named after him.

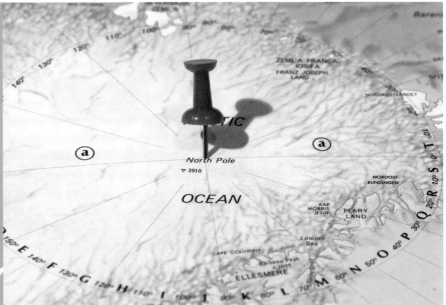

UNDERSTANDING OUR PAST

As human beings, we have always been driven by the need to understand who we are and where we came from. Amazing scientific achievements have been made in discovering the answers to these questions.

DARWIN AND EVOLUTION

Charles Darwin was a British **naturalist**. From 1831 to 1836, he sailed around the world on a ship called the *HMS Beagle*, collecting and studying plants and animals to better understand the natural world. These studies led him to develop his theory of **natural selection**, which states that animals who are better suited to their environments are more likely to survive and pass their characteristics on to their **offspring**. This is also called "survival of the fittest." Darwin realized that natural selection can lead to a whole species changing slowly over time, or even develop into a new species. This led to his theory of **evolution**, which explains how long ago humans evolved from a type of ape.

Charles Darwin

THE HUMAN GENOME PROJECT

Scientists have learned much about who we are, but perhaps their most important discovery has been the ability to understand how our genes work. Genes are small strands of **DNA** that contain the instructions for the creation of all living things. From eye color to height to how we think, every part of us is determined by our genes.

All the genes of a living thing put together is called its **genome**. If you think of DNA as letters, and genes as the sentences, the genome is the entire book. In 1990, scientists around the world began the work of reading and understanding every gene in the human genome.

DNA strand

In 2003, 13 years later, the last genes were **decoded** and the human genome was completely understood for the first time. This incredible achievement means we have the ability to understand our bodies and how we evolved better than ever before. Based on this knowledge, scientists can now go on to develop new medicines and treatments.

SUPERHUMANS IN SPORTS

Humans have always enjoyed pushing themselves and their bodies to the limit, competing to be the fastest, strongest, or simply the best. Here are some of the greatest sports achievements of all time.

USAIN BOLT: FASTEST HUMAN EVER

Usain Bolt is the greatest sprinter of all time. He holds the world records in the 100-meter and 200-meter races, and as part of the 400-meter relay team. He is the only sprinter to win the 100 meter and 200 meter at three **consecutive** Olympic Games, known as the "Triple Double."

In 1935, Jesse Owens set three new world records and tied a fourth in less than one hour: the 100-yard dash, the long jump, the 220-yard sprint, and the 220-yard low hurdles. The following year, Owens won four gold medals at the 1936 Berlin Olympic Games.

There are almost as many amazing achievements as there are different sports. Who are your sports heroes?

JESSE OWENS: FOUR RECORDS IN AN HOUR

STEFFI GRAF: NUMBER ONE

No other tennis player has held the world number one spot as long as Steffi Graf. She spent 377 weeks as the best-ranked player in the world. She is also the only player ever to win the "Golden Slam," when she won all four **Grand Slam** singles titles plus Olympic gold in the same year.

NADIA COMANECI: PERFECT TEN

At only 14 years old, Nadia Comaneci became the first ever gymnast to be awarded a perfect score of 10 in the 1976 Olympic Games. Comaneci is also the youngest ever gymnastics all-around champion, and due to changes in the age limits, this will never be broken. She is most famous for being the first gymnast to receive seven perfect 10 scores at the Olympics.

ROGER BANNISTER: THE FOUR-MINUTE MILE

For a long time, it was thought that it was impossible for any human to run 1 mile (1.6 km) in less than four minutes. On May 6, 1954, at the Iffley Road track in Oxford, England, Roger Bannister ran it in 3 minutes and 59.4 seconds, proving everyone wrong!

TRISCHA ZORN: PARALYMPIC LEGEND

Trischa Zorn was born blind. However, she didn't let this stop her winning the most **Paralympic** medals of any athlete ever: 41 gold, 9 silver, and 5 bronze—55 in total!

LINES OF COMMUNICATION

TALKING ON THE TELEPHONE

Alexander Graham Bell was born in 1847 in Edinburgh, Scotland. His mother and his wife were deaf, which partly inspired Bell to study speech and different types of communication. He went on to make history by inventing one of the earliest versions of the telephone and using that telephone to make the first ever telephone call.

When Bell's job was to experiment on **telegraph wires**, he became interested in the idea of **transmitting** human voices rather than messages over wires. Together with his partner, Thomas Watson, the two developed a device to make Bell's idea become a reality. They invented the telephone.

Alexander Graham Bell

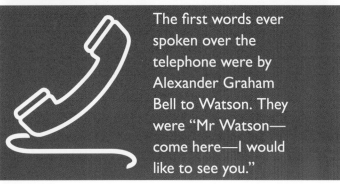

The first words ever spoken over the telephone were by Alexander Graham Bell to Watson. They were "Mr Watson—come here—I would like to see you."

What would YOU have said?

INVENTING THE WORLD WIDE WEB

The World Wide Web was officially invented in 1989. An English man, Tim Berners-Lee, was working for a company and found it frustrating that he had to get different information from different computers, each using a different program that he had to learn. He had an idea to create one system on which all people could access all information at all times. Berners-Lee turned his idea into a reality and created the World Wide Web.

Tim Berners-Lee

Berners-Lee created an information space where people could access and share documents, images, videos, and audio files. This space, the Internet, has allowed people to communicate much more easily with one another and access huge amounts of information. Nowadays, we can use the Internet to do practically everything—to order food, to buy clothes, and even to help us do our homework!

VACCINES AND ANTIBIOTICS

VACCINES

Edward Jenner knew that **milkmaids**, who often caught cowpox from cows, did not catch smallpox, a deadly disease. He realized that cowpox must make someone **immune** to smallpox. To test his theory, Jenner infected a small boy, James Phipps, with cowpox. Phipps became ill, but recovered. When Jenner tried to give him smallpox, Phipps did not catch the disease. This process was named vaccination.

Later, a scientist named Louis Pasteur attempted to find a cure for **typhoid** fever, after losing three of his children to the disease. He worked on animals first, and learned that by giving a weaker form of a disease to an animal, he could help their bodies learn to fight the disease, making them immune. This was the beginning of modern vaccines.

Vaccines help to prevent diseases. Thanks to vaccines, the disease called smallpox was wiped out.

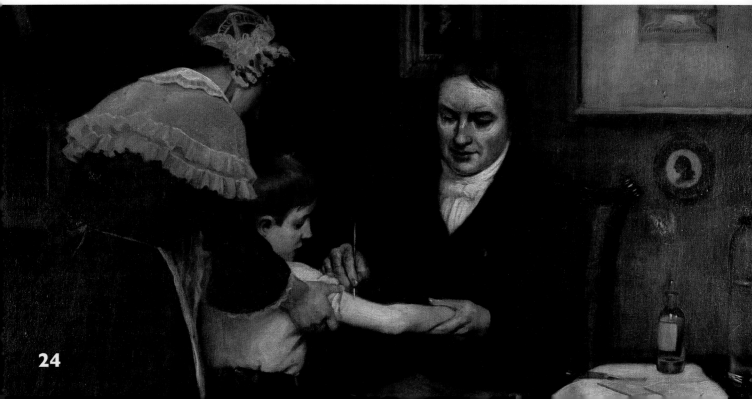

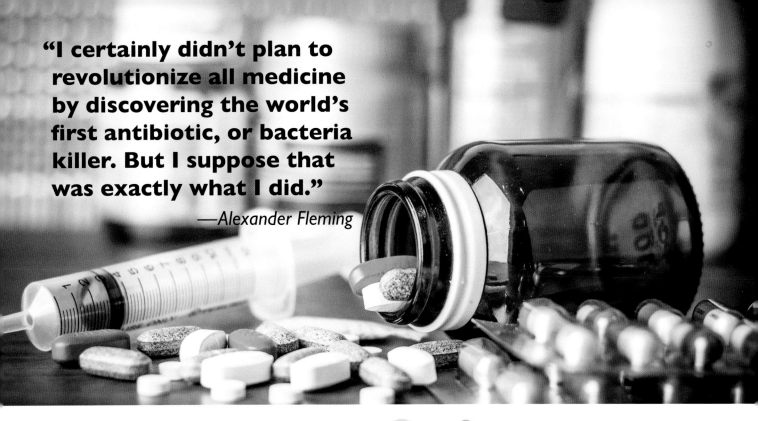

> **"I certainly didn't plan to revolutionize all medicine by discovering the world's first antibiotic, or bacteria killer. But I suppose that was exactly what I did."**
>
> —*Alexander Fleming*

ANTIBIOTICS

Before bacteria were discovered, people used medicines without really knowing how they worked. Some scientists, including Pasteur, had noticed that certain types of mold did not get **contaminated** with bacteria. An Italian doctor, Vincenzo Tiberio, and a student, Ernest Duchesne, had been working on this idea, but in 1928, it was Sir Alexander Fleming who made a significant breakthrough.

Fleming had been researching a type of bacteria. When he went on vacation with his family, he left some samples of the bacteria lying on a bench. After returning from his vacation, he noticed that one had gone moldy. When he looked closer, he realized that the mold had killed all the bacteria! Fleming did some experiments on the mold, called penicillin, and created the world's first antibiotic—a medicine to kill bacteria. Today, antibiotics can be used to treat and cure many different diseases, revolutionizing the world of medicine.

Sir Alexander Fleming

BREAKING THE LIMITS

Human beings like to go fast. Really fast. We have learned to move faster than our bodies will allow by developing machines such as cars, motorcycles, and airplanes. Human beings have always wanted to push the limits of what can be achieved. Technology is helping us travel faster than we ever have before.

THE FASTEST ON LAND

The fastest vehicle recorded on land (so far) was the ThrustSSC, or Thrust **Supersonic** Car. The ThrustSSC is a British jet-propelled car developed by Richard Noble, Glynne Bowsher, Ron Ayres, and Jeremy Bliss. It set the land speed record on October 15, 1997, achieving a speed of 763 mph (1,228 kph). It was also the first vehicle to break the sound barrier on land, which means it traveled faster than the speed of sound!

Spirit of Australia

ThrustSSC

THE FASTEST IN THE WATER

The fastest vehicle on water is currently the *Spirit of Australia*. Ken Warby set the record on October 8, 1978 in New South Wales, Australia. The *Spirit of Australia* had an average speed of 318 mph (511 kph). The record has not yet been broken, although two official attempts have been made. The water speed record is very dangerous. As many as 85 percent of people who attempt the record die in the attempt.

THE FASTEST IN THE AIR

Since the Wright brothers first took off, planes and jets have become faster and faster. The SR-71 Blackbird holds the current record for the fastest manned, airbreathing jet aircraft. Airbreathing means the jet engines take in air and use that to create **thrust**. The SR-71 officially reached a speed of **Mach** 3.3, which is more than 2,530 mph (4,075 kph)!

When a space shuttle takes off, it has to reach incredible speeds to break out of Earth's atmosphere and get into **orbit**. Its engines use burning fuel to create the hot gases it needs to go so fast. The fastest space shuttle takeoff achieved so far is around 17,400 mph (28,000 kph).

HUMANITY'S FARTHEST JOURNEY

• • • • • • • • • • • • • • • • • •

In the late 1970s, NASA launched its most ambitious program yet. At that time, the planets Jupiter, Saturn, Uranus, and Neptune were **aligned**, something that only occurs every 176 years. So NASA created two **probes** to visit each planet. They are named Voyager 1 and Voyager 2. The two identical probes were launched in 1977. Today, the probes are still flying and collecting data. Voyager 1's power is expected to last until 2021, and Voyager 2's until 2020.

Voyager 2 is the only spacecraft to have visited Uranus and Neptune.

 Voyager 1 discovered active volcanoes on Jupiter's moon, Io.

 Voyager 2 measured the temperature on Uranus at -357°F (-216°C), making it the coldest place in the solar system!

Neptune, as captured by Voyager 2 in 1989.

On February 14, 1990, Voyager 1 captured an image of Earth as it entered the edge of our solar system. Earth can be seen as a tiny dot (see right). This photo was taken from more than 3.7 billion miles (6 billion km) away.

Both Voyager probes were packed with a Golden Record. Each disc contains information about Earth, including greetings in 55 languages, photographs, and a selection of music. It is hoped that, if found by other life forms, they will be able to learn about Earth from the Golden Record.

"Consider again that dot. That's here. That's home. That's us. On it everyone you love, everyone you know, everyone you ever heard of, every human being who ever was, lived out their lives…on a mote of dust suspended on a sunbeam."
—Carl Sagan, Voyager Scientist

Earth

Voyager 2 captured this image of Saturn's rings in 1981.

GLOSSARY

aligned Arranged in a straight line

allegedly Describing something that is claimed to be true, but not proven

altitudes The height of an object in relation to sea level or ground level

barren A place where nothing can grow or live

chapel A place of Christian worship

consecutive One after another

contaminated Made unclean by the addition of a poisonous substance

DNA Short for deoxyribonucleic acid, the genetic information located inside the cells of all living things

decode To break down information into a form that is understandable

dictatorship A form of government in which one person makes all of the decisions for a country

evolution The theory that all living things developed from earlier living things

expedition A journey for a specific purpose

feats Amazing achievements

fresco A painting done on moist plaster

genome A living thing's complete set of genetic information

Grand Slam The winning of all major championships in a sport in the same year

immune To be resistant to illness or disease

knighted To be recognized and given a rank, typically by the British monarch

Mach The speed of something compared to the speed of sound

milkmaid In the past, a girl or woman who milked cows

natural selection The theory that nature favors the healthiest living thing to survive and reproduce

naturalist A person who studies the natural world

neutral To not take a side in a disagreement

offspring The child or young of a living thing

orbit The path that an object makes around a larger object in space

Paralympics A major sporting competition for athletes with disabilities

LEARNING MORE

• • • • • • • • • • • • • • • • • • • •

plateau A high area of land or ice

principle A basic law or truth on which an action or behavior is based

probe An instrument, tool, or spacecraft used to explore other planets

Roman Catholic A branch of Christianity

scaffold A temporary structure that keeps something in place

sculptor A person who creates artworks such as statues

Sherpa Tibetan people in Nepal known for their mountain-climbing expertise

summit The highest part of a mountain

supersonic To travel faster than the speed of sound

telegraph wires A system used to send messages electronically across long distances

thrust A force that pushes something forward

transmit To send or carry from one place to another

typhoid An infectious bacterial disease transmitted by water

BOOKS

Bow, James. *Space Entrepreneurs*. Crabtree Publishing, 2018.

Ipellie, Alootook. *The Inuit Thought of It: Amazing Arctic Innovations*. Annick Press, 2007.

O'Brien, Cynthia. *Innovations in Communication*. Crabtree Publishing, 2017.

WEBSITES

Learn more about the Moon landing here: **https://kids.nationalgeographic. com/explore/history/moon- landing/**

Check out this site for fun facts, photos, and videos about the North and South Pole: **https://kids.nationalgeographic. com/explore/nature/habitats/ polar/#emperor-penguin-chicks.jpg**

Visit this site to learn more about the Voyager program: **https://www.ouruniverseforkids. com/voyager-1/**

INDEX

• • • • • • • • • • • • • • • • • •